"TOO SMART" JONES

and the
Mysterious
Artist

"TOO SMART" JONES and the Mysterious Artist **JONES**

10

A GILBERT MORRIS MYSTERY

MOODY PRESS
CHICAGO

ISBN: 0-8024-4034-7

1 3 5 7 9 10 8 6 4 2

Printed in the United States of America

Contents

1

The Fence

Juliet "Too Smart" Jones stood waiting with her friends, the other homeschooled boys and girls. They were all about to start on their newest community project. Juliet was ten years old. She was not wearing her big horn-rimmed glasses today, and the green T-shirt she had on was her favorite. She also had on a pair of light tan shorts and Nike running shoes. She was ready to go to work.

Behind Juliet stood her brother, Joe. He was nine, but he was already three inches taller than she was. He would be a big man someday. He had red hair and blue eyes exactly like his father's (and he was rather proud of that). At the moment he was waving his arms excitedly and explaining his latest invention to Flash Gordon, who was sitting in his wheelchair beside him.

Juliet felt a pang of sadness for Flash. His real name wasn't Flash, of course. His name was Melvin. Before that car accident last year hurt his legs, he had been the fastest runner of all the boys. He was usually cheerful, though, and he had learned how to play several sports well while in his wheelchair.

Waiting, Juliet listened to their conversation with only half an ear.

Joe was saying eagerly, "So what this new invention will do is put an alarm system on a bicycle." His eyes grew bright, and he waved his arms even more as he talked. "Everybody knows that a car with an alarm is safer than one that hasn't one. People don't steal cars with alarms. So what I'm making is this alarm that will go on a bicycle. A thief takes the bike, and—*bam!*—it goes off. I've been thinking I might even put an electric system on it. It would send an electric shock that'll knock the bicycle thief down flat."

Juliet heard Flash groan, and she smiled.

Flash said, "No doubt about it, Joe. You're going to be rich and famous someday. You got more ideas in your head than anybody I ever heard of. Someday one of them's going to work."

"What do you mean one of them's going to work!" Joe was indignant. "A lot of my inventions have worked. I'm insulted that you'd even say that!"

"Name one of your inventions that's really

worked," Flash said. "And don't tell me about the paint mixer you made that blew green and purple paint all over your folks' living room."

"Well, that one did have a little bug in it. But I'm going to fix it when I get time." Then Joe said. "Hey, what do you say after this meeting's over we go play basketball in the park?"

Juliet thought Flash was quiet an extralong time. He finally said, "I guess you better count me out this time." He sounded . . . sad?

Juliet turned around to look at Flash. She was rather puzzled, for he was usually so cheerful about everything. But she saw that indeed he did look sad today.

"What's the matter, Flash?" she asked him. "Don't you feel good today?"

"Oh, sure. I feel OK."

"You look a little down."

"Aw, it's just that—well, sometimes I get to thinking about when I could run with the rest of the guys, and now I can't. And I wish I could. And—"

"I know it must be tough."

"I don't want to complain. I think the Lord's going to get me out of this chair someday, but I wish it was *now*. I sort of wish He'd hurry."

Juliet said, "Our family is praying—well, everybody's praying—that your legs will get well soon and that you'll be able to walk and run again."

Flash managed a smile. "I know, and I appreciate it. That would be wonderful, and I know God's able to do it. But the doctor isn't very hopeful."

Juliet was about to say something encouraging to Flash, but at that moment Mrs. Winfred Boyd called all the homeschoolers to order. "I think we're about ready to go now," she said. "We have it all straight, do we? Are there any questions?"

"I've got a question."

Juliet sighed. Billy Rollins *always* had a question. He was a loud boy, just her age, and she'd always thought he was rather obnoxious.

"I don't see why we have to clean up the mess that somebody else made," Billy grumbled.

Mrs. Boyd waved her finger at him. "Billy Rollins, I'm surprised at you! You know that we want to make our town as beautiful as we possibly can. So we've got to work at it."

Mrs. Boyd herself had thought up this community project for the Oakwood youngsters who were taught at home by their parents.

Juliet couldn't help whispering to Flash over her shoulder. "I'm with Billy on this one for a change. I don't see why we have to clean up the graffiti that some people have put all over town. What's the matter with people, anyway?"

"I guess some folks are just naturally ornery," Flash murmured quietly. "They don't care how bad they make things look."

But now Mrs. Boyd was talking again. "We have all the materials you will need. We have paint for you to use to paint over some of the bad graffiti, and we have a paint roller for everyone, and buckets." She paused, wrinkled her forehead thoughtfully, and then said, "Now, sometimes you're going to see some rude words that people have painted on a fence or the side of a building. But I don't want you to look at them. Just take your paint rollers and paint over them."

Chili Williams waved his hand wildly. "How we gonna paint over 'em if we can't see 'em, Mrs. Boyd?"

"Just keep your eyes shut until you've gotten them covered up with paint," Mrs. Boyd said firmly, and she started toward the cars.

"That'll be quite a trick," Chili Williams said, grinning. He walked over to his best friend, Flash Gordon. "Ready to go, buddy?"

"I guess I am."

Chili frowned down at him and then glanced questioningly at Juliet.

She was quite sure he was thinking exactly what she was— *Flash doesn't seem himself today.*

"We'll make the cleanup real fun," Chili announced. "Let's show 'em how to do it, Flash."

The Boyds' van and a couple of cars first took the homeschoolers to a fence that had been covered with vulgar pictures and bad language. Everybody got out. The adults unloaded the buckets and the rollers and the paint.

"We're going to paint right over this one," Mrs. Boyd said. "Let's see how quickly we can get the job done. And no looking at the pictures."

Actually the paint job turned out to be rather fun. Because the buckets of paint were large and they used rollers, the work did go fast. Besides, a lot of shouting and teasing went on as they painted.

Joe found himself working beside Billy Rollins. Slyly he dripped a few paint drops on Billy's hand.

Just as he expected, Billy let out a holler and made a swipe at Joe's face with his roller. Joe was too quick for him, though. He ducked and ran away.

Billy Rollins took off after him.

They raced up and down the fence until Mrs. Tanner stopped them both. She said in a firm voice, "That's it. No playing around! Go back to work, Billy. You too, Joe."

They did.

Farther down the old fence, Juliet and Chili Williams were having a good time rolling on the paint. Once Juliet just stood scowling at the messed-up fence, though. She said, "I just can't understand why anyone would even want to put mean things like this on somebody else's fence."

"I don't either," Chili said. "Seems like the world's got enough bad stuff in it already without making it worse." He glanced across to where Flash was sitting in his wheelchair, slowly dabbing away at the fence. "Something's really got Flash upset today," he said.

"I know it," Juliet agreed. "He's just not himself."

"Usually he's the most cheerful guy I know. Something big is on his mind."

Juliet made another sweep with her paint roller. "See if you can find out what's bothering him."

A little later, Juliet found herself working side by side with her brother. The fence was almost finished now, but Joe had started to fuss. It was just awful, he complained, that the Oakwood Support Group had to waste their good time cleaning up other people's messes.

"It sure is," she agreed. "I keep wondering who could be doing this."

Joe seemed to think he heard something different in his sister's voice. He stopped painting. Then he planted himself in front of Juliet, looked directly into her eyes, and said, "And what are you thinking about?"

"Me? Why, nothing. Except that I still keep wondering what kind of people would do something like this."

"Don't give me that! I know you got something special on your mind."

"I'm just getting bored, I guess. This is work that has to be done, but it's gotten really boring."

Joe continued to ask questions, but she wouldn't talk anymore about the fence painters. She just kept on thinking about them.

Actually, Juliet's mind was running at a rapid rate. For a long time, some friends—and others—had been calling her "Too Smart Jones." They did that because she was very good at her schoolwork. But she was also called "Sherlock Holmes" by Joe. That was because she wanted to be a detective someday. She loved to dabble in mysteries or puzzles of any kind.

And as Juliet continued to paint, she began planning a way to find out who was painting this disgusting graffiti. At one point she even stopped painting, reached into her back pocket, and took out a little notebook. She brought a pencil out of her shirt pocket and began to write some things that occurred to her.

Suddenly a hand appeared before her face, and she snatched the notebook away. As she had suspected, Joe was reaching for it. "Get away, Joe. This is a private notebook. Private information."

"I just want to know what you're doing. I know it's something."

Juliet sighed. "You are absolutely the

nosiest boy I ever saw! All right. All right. I just want to see if we can find some way to catch the boys who are doing this to buildings and fences."

Flash was at work on the other side of Juliet. He gave her a look and said, "How do you know it's boys?"

"You don't think *girls* would do a thing like this, do you?"

"I know some that might," Chili Williams piped up from the other side of Flash. He grinned over at her.

"So now I suppose we're into another great mystery," Joe said and let out a loud groan. "Sherlock Holmes here—alias Too Smart Jones—is in charge again."

"It's nothing like that!" Juliet protested. "Nothing like that at all. But I do want to see if we can find out who's doing all this stuff."

"So we'll help you." Surprisingly, Chili Williams came around Flash and stood at attention in front of her. "Give us our orders," he said.

Juliet thought a moment longer. "Then, let's all of us meet tomorrow, and we'll get Jenny and Samuel and Delores together with us."

"What'll we do when we're all together?" Joe asked. "Eat something, I hope."

Juliet couldn't help smiling at that. Her brother was always thinking of food. "We probably will," she told him. "Everybody bring some money, and we'll go to the ice cream shop and talk about this for a while—and have some ice cream."

"*Then* what are we going to do?"

"Split up and go all over town and take notes on what kind of writings we see on fences and buildings and things. That's what we'll do. We've got to find a clue or two before we can solve this mystery."

2

Detectives at Work

Juliet and Joe were used to spending every weekday morning at their studies. Their father had made a spare room into a classroom for them, and their mother worked with them on their lessons. Usually they were finished by noon, and after a quick lunch they would leave the house for some free time.

The afternoon after the homeschool painting project, they got on their bicycles and raced down to the ice cream shop. There they found their friends already gathered around a table impatiently waiting for them.

Beside Flash Gordon and Chili Williams, the group today included Samuel and Delores Del Rio. Samuel was eleven, and Delores was nine. They both were very good at gymnastics, for their parents had been aerialists in a circus. Samuel and Delores now lived with

Grandmother and Grandfather Del Rio in a nice, big old house on the edge of town. Jenny White, Juliet's best friend, was at the ice cream shop, too. She was a red-haired nine-year-old.

Juliet thought they might wait for ice cream until after they had done their clue-hunting, but Joe said, "I've got a better idea than that. We'll have ice cream before *and* after." So Juliet gave in, and Joe looked very pleased with himself for having come up with that idea.

Within minutes, everyone was sitting at the table, spooning in ice cream.

For a while they talked about the cleanup they did yesterday. They took guesses at who could be responsible for the rude remarks on the old fence.

Then Jenny began to ask one question after another.

"So what are we going to do, Juliet? I still don't know exactly what we are looking for."

Juliet had prepared sheets of guidelines using their classroom computer. Now she took them from her satchel and passed them out.

"You see, at the top is where you put the date. Then below that you put the location—that's *where* did you see the writing or the pictures or whatever it was."

"Oh, I get it!" Joe chirped, with a wink at Chili Williams. "Location—that means where we are. Is that right?"

"I'm not sure I understand," Chili said, winking back at Joe. "Go over it one more time, Juliet."

Juliet knew the boys loved to tease her about being so fussy with her detecting methods. She just sniffed and ignored them. "Then over here in this column you put what *kind* of graffiti it was."

"But what if it's bad words?" Chili asked. "Are we supposed to write those down? I don't think my folks would like me writing bad words—even for a good reason."

Juliet hesitated over that. A frown came to her forehead. "Maybe you'd better just write down 'bad words.' Or 'bad picture.'"

But clearly Chili was in a teasing mood today. "But there are all kinds of bad words," he said. "Some are just a little bit bad, some are medium bad, and some are horrible bad."

"Then write that down! A little bad, medium bad, or horrible bad," Juliet told him impatiently.

"What are we hoping to find?" Flash asked. He had a vanilla milkshake and was still slowly sipping it.

"We're going to try and find out where these awful people are located."

"Oh yeah. Located. That means where they are? Right?" Chili Williams joked.

"Just be quiet, Chili!" Juliet said. "Don't you see? If we find that the same people are writing this stuff in a certain area, we can stake it out. "

"A steak out—I'd have T-bone. That's my favorite steak." Chili wouldn't settle down.

"Ribeye for me," Joe joined in. "I like to have a steak out in the open every once in a while." Juliet's brother loved bad jokes, and he laughed loudly at his own humor.

Even Flash, who still had been acting rather gloomy so far, laughed at this.

Juliet ignored them all. "Here we go, then," she said. "Is everybody finished with your ice cream?"

"Not me!" Joe said. "I never get finished with ice cream! I don't think there's enough ice cream in the whole world to make me completely happy."

But they left the ice cream shop anyway and started making their rounds.

Juliet had assigned herself the northeast part of Oakwood. It was not the best part of town or the worst, either. She made notes as she walked along. From time to time she would even jot down a description of certain people she saw on the way. Soon her little notebook was getting full.

"The words on this building are horrible bad," she muttered to herself. "It's too bad that children have to see them."

She moved steadily along the sidewalk, walking to the north. She soon discovered that she was not seeing a lot of bad graffiti in this direction. What she did begin to find was just different-colored shapes sprayed on the sides of buildings.

Then she ran into Flash. He was coming back from covering another area. "What did you find out, Flash?"

"There wasn't so much bad stuff where I was looking," he reported. He showed her his tablet. "But what I did find was a lot of hearts with initials inside."

Juliet studied the tablet, then said, "Well, we're beginning to get a pattern as to where the bad stuff is."

"I guess we are."

"Flash, you just aren't yourself today. You still feeling down?"

Flash Gordon managed a smile. "Aw, I don't mean to be discouraged and doubting the Lord, but I've been asking Him to heal me for a long time now. My parents have been praying, and other people have been praying, and I'm still not any better."

Juliet suddenly felt very sorry for Flash. "Sometimes people have to pray a long time before God does what they ask for," she told him. "I read about a man who prayed for three friends to be saved for over fifty years."

"And did they get saved?"

"Not one of them did while he was alive.

And then they all became Christians a year after he died."

"You mean he prayed for something for fifty years and he never got to see the answer?"

"Never did. The book I read said he probably did see it from heaven, though."

Flash suddenly grinned, and for a moment he looked like his old self. "Hey, Juliet, you're a real good friend. You know how to make a guy feel better. Now let's get on with solving this mystery."

Side by side, the two of them started back toward the ice cream shop. Before long they met up with the others, doing the same thing.

The first thing Joe said was, "So let's go and have some more ice cream while we compare what we found."

"That sounds like a winner to me," Chili said. "I've walked off about ten pounds. I need strength."

They were getting close to the ice cream parlor street when Juliet happened to glance down an alley. She stopped. "What's that down there?"

"What's what?" Flash asked.

"I thought I saw some something down in the alley," Juliet said, frowning. "Some bright color you don't usually see in an alley. Let's go check it out." She started down the alleyway.

She heard the others following her. She heard Flash, rolling along in his wheelchair.

It was a little dark in the narrow alley, but

Juliet had no trouble seeing what she had noticed from the street.

"Well, look at that!" Flash breathed from behind her. "Isn't that something!"

"It sure is!" Joe joined in. "Never saw anything like that before!"

Juliet stood staring as the others commented on what they all saw. A painting adorned the side of the old brick building. The colors in the painting were so believable, and the painting was so large, that she said softly, "That makes me feel like I'm right at the beach!"

"Me too," Chili Williams agreed. "Look at that green water. It's even got whitecaps. And see—there's bigger waves coming up behind them. It's just like the ocean."

Jenny touched the painting, and her eyes were large. "Look at that! There's dolphins out there. I've been to the ocean, and that's just the way they look. Just like they're dancing."

Then Chili pointed at the top of the painting. "What kind of birds are those?" he asked.

"Seagulls," Juliet told him.

Chili kept staring at the painted birds. Then he said, "I wonder if they're good to eat?"

"No, I don't think so." Juliet had to laugh. "I think they'd taste fishy."

They all stood looking for some time. Juliet still could not believe her eyes. She loved paintings, and she knew that what someone had painted on the brick wall here was very good.

As the others were talking among themselves, still looking, Juliet was thinking and making notes in her notebook. *Now I've got two mysteries to solve. One is, who's spray-painting the bad words and pictures? And two is, who's the mysterious artist who's done this beautiful work?*

"You know what I think?" Flash said suddenly. "I'd really rather find out who this good artist is than find out who's doing all the bad words."

Juliet smiled. "You're thinking just what I was thinking. But maybe we can do both."

"Kind of sad to think that this won't be here long. Somebody else will come along and draw dirty pictures or write bad words on it and mess it up," Joe said. "It's too bad that you can't just take it off the brick wall. I'd like to have it in my bedroom."

Juliet said quick as a flash, "If we can find the artist, we'll tell him that he ought to paint pictures like this on canvas. Then he could sell them."

"That's a good idea, all right," Flash said, "but how are we going to find him?"

"I'm not sure right now." Juliet frowned as she thought. "But we're going to try. Let's go down to the library and see if there are any books in there about a local artist who paints like this."

"Sure, we can do that," Joe said. But then he added firmly, "*After* we have our ice cream!"

3

The Mysterious Artist

Juliet and Joe's classroom was upstairs in the Jones house. It was cluttered from one end to the other. Maps, diagrams, and charts covered the walls. The tops of the desks were covered, and the shelves that their father had built them were stuffed with old projects. Joe's inventions, such as they were, took up a great deal of the space.

Their study area was even more crowded than usual today, for Juliet had been to the local library. Most of the books she had checked out were very large ones. Joe had noticed that all were about paintings and sculptures. She seemed to think that thumbing through them was an exciting thing to do.

Joe himself was not interested in art books. He watched her for a while, and he made a comment from time to time. When she ignored him, he began rolling up pieces of paper. Taking careful aim, he sailed one through the air. It stuck in her hair, and she brushed at it. Maybe she thought it was Boots, her cat, pawing at her hair. Boots did that sometimes.

Joe stifled a laugh and made a larger paper wad. It took several, but finally Juliet stopped brushing at her hair. She looked up and saw him preparing to launch another missile.

"You stop that, Joe Jones!"

"I'm working on a new invention," he said. "I have to figure out the arc of a paper wad before it hits the head of a sister who's too smart."

Juliet jumped up from her desk and ran toward him. She snatched at the paper wad in his hand. He held it out of her reach, and she threw herself on him. They both fell sprawling on the floor. The chair went over with a crash.

"Get off of me!" Joe yelled.

"I will not!" Juliet screamed back, equally loud. She was still making wild grabs for the paper wad.

Then they bumped into the floor lamp, and it toppled over with a crash. Unfortunately, that broke the bulb.

"What in the world are you two doing?"

Joe looked toward the door. There stood their mother with her hands on her hips. She had a stern look on her face, too, and she was shaking her head with displeasure, the way she sometimes did. "This doesn't look like studying to me!"

"Well, it's all his fault!" Juliet cried, getting to her feet. "He's been throwing paper wads at me!"

"Joe, did you do that?"

Since there were paper wads all over the floor by Juliet's desk, Joe could hardly deny that he had.

"I was just working on an invention."

"He was not. He was just being awful."

"Joe, I'm going to give you ten more math problems. Apparently you don't have enough to do."

Joe yelped. "Not that! Anything but that!"

Mrs. Jones did not give in. "Don't even talk to me about it."

Joe began to protest loudly anyway.

But their mom said, "I don't want to hear anything else about this. Not one thing."

"But she was just looking at books on painting. I *hate* books on painting!"

"Well, I think maybe we might find a different approach to art that might be more helpful than throwing paper wads. I know of one."

"What kind of approach, Mom?" Juliet asked, interest in her voice.

Joe groaned. He knew Juliet not only liked to look at the pictures but even to read the stories about the paintings. And she was always ready for something "different."

"They're going to have a big display of art over at the museum in Collinsville. I thought we could all go over there and look at it."

"Oh, Mom, that would be wonderful!"

"I don't see what's so wonderful about it. I know what those art displays are. Just a bunch of pictures and statues," Joe complained.

"Joe, you need to learn to open your mind to things. Besides, we're all going."

"Who is all?" he grumbled.

"All of your friends in the Support Group."

"I bet we'll see some of the pictures that I found in these books," Juliet said excitedly.

"You may. And it'll be fun," Mrs. Jones said with a smile. "Now, Joe, let me give you these extra problems." Ignoring his wails, she opened the book and made the assignment.

The trip to Collinsville was fun, just as Juliet had expected. The weather was beautiful, and they got to the museum just in time to get in. Their sponsors for the day were Mrs. Jones and Mrs. Tanner.

Before they went inside, Mrs. Tanner said, "Now, I want you to behave yourselves. We're going in as a group, and I don't want any horseplay. Not from anybody. Especially not from you, Billy."

Billy Rollins rolled his eyes. "Why are you always picking on me?"

"Because you're always the ringleader in any kind of trouble," Flash said with a grin.

Juliet soon decided that this field trip actually was one of the most interesting tours they had ever taken. She saw a few of the paintings she'd seen in the art books, and she recognized them at once.

"Look at this goofy one," Billy Rollins said loudly. He'd stopped and was pointing at a painting that consisted mostly of circles and squares in different colors. "That doesn't look like anything."

"That's modern art," Juliet said importantly. "It's from the cubist school of art."

"I could do that myself," Billy said. "I wonder how much that guy got paid for doing this."

"Fifty thousand dollars," said the pleasant-faced lady who was taking them around on the tour. "And that's one of his less expensive paintings."

They all looked at the painting for a while. Nobody said he liked it.

Chili Williams said, "I'm gonna grow up and be a painter. I could knock this out in twenty minutes and have me fifty thousand bucks to buy me a Jaguar with."

"I'm afraid it's not that easy," the museum guide said. Then she went on to talk for some time about how some art is not a picture of anything. "You can recognize a tree, or a scene in the country, or a building," she said. "But other kinds of art are like this one."

Billy Rollins still scoffed. "Fifty thousand dollars. What a rip-off. Anybody could do that!"

After the interesting tour, they went to a fast-food place, where they had hamburgers, french fries, and milkshakes.

Juliet sat by Flash as they were eating. They began talking about the mystery artist who had painted the beautiful picture in the alley.

"I've been thinking, Flash," she said. "If we could just find this wonderful artist, maybe he could paint scenes like that on the walls in *all* the alleys. That would make our town beautiful."

"How do you know it's a he?" Flash grinned broadly. "Maybe it's a girl."

The idea had not occurred to Juliet, but she nodded at once. "Maybe it is. But usually girls don't hang out in alleys." Then she noticed that Flash was rubbing the tops of his legs. She wondered if he was uncomfortable. "Are your legs hurting you?"

"No, not really," Flash said. "They just feel funny today."

"We're still praying for you. Flash. One of these days you're going to be running down that court and dunking a basketball. You'll be a big star! You'll see."

Flash found a smile. "Thanks a lot, Juliet. I know you're right, if that's what God wants."

The trip home was noisy because Billy Rollins and Samuel Del Rio got into a big argument. Neither one particularly liked to be wrong, so Mrs. Tanner finally had to command them sternly to keep absolutely silent.

Juliet was talking to Flash again about what they had found. "Maybe we could go to the newspaper and tell them about the picture in the alley. If we get a little publicity, we might be able to find the mysterious artist."

"The mysterious artist. Is that what you're going to call him?"

"I guess so. He is mysterious, isn't he?"

Flash grinned. "Another mystery. You never get enough of mysteries. When you're an old lady in a nursing home, you'll be solving mysteries, Too Smart Jones."

4

Junkyard Jake

Juliet's mother came into the kitchen while Juliet and Joe were still eating breakfast. She had the morning newspaper in her hand. "I think you two would be interested in taking a look at this."

Juliet glanced up from her cereal. "What is it, Mom?"

"You're going to be surprised!" Mrs. Jones exclaimed. She lay the paper flat on the table, then asked with delight in her voice, "Now, what about *that!*"

Juliet looked at the front page, and her eyes flew open wide. "Joe! See? It's the very same picture we found in the alley, isn't it?"

He snatched up the newspaper. "Let me see that!"

"Joe, don't grab things like that. It's not polite," their mother protested. "Be more mannerly."

"Well, I just wanted to see." He held the paper in both hands and stared at the front page. His eyes were big. "It's the same one, all right."

Juliet finally got her hands on the newspaper. She looked thoughtfully at the picture and said, "It's not in color here, but it's the same picture. I didn't think they would put it on the front page, though!"

"What's so newsy about a picture in an alley?" Joe asked. "I wonder why they printed it in the newspaper at all."

"Because I went by the newspaper office and told them the picture was there. And that it was beautiful. See—somebody's written a story to go with the picture. It's called 'Mysterious Artist Comes to Oakwood.'"

She began reading aloud. Then she stopped and said proudly, "Look here—my name's in the paper. 'Juliet Jones has brought this matter to our attention, and we are grateful to her.' That's what it says."

"You're famous," her brother said with a big grin.

Juliet made a face at him.

Today was Saturday. They would have no schoolwork to do this morning. Juliet and Joe finished breakfast.

"What are you two going to do today?" Mrs. Jones asked as she and Juliet cleared away the breakfast dishes. She always told people that Juliet was very good at helping with the housework.

"Oh, we're just going to go down to the park and shoot some baskets and play softball maybe," Joe said.

"And I might go over to the Del Rios'," Juliet said, "and play with Delores for a while."

Juliet and Joe had just started down the street on their bikes when they saw Jenny and Delores pedaling toward them. The girls reported that Samuel and the other boys had already left to look for clues on their own.

"That's what they said anyhow," Jenny told them. "They'll probably wind up doing nothing but playing games."

"I'll tell you what let's do—" Juliet began. But she had no chance to finish.

"I'm going after the guys!" Joe exclaimed. "I don't want to look for clues with a bunch of girls."

"It might do you good to stay with us," Juliet said. "You might get a little culture."

"I'd rather have a corny dog." He started to pedal away. "Who needs culture, anyway?"

"We'll meet at the ice cream shop at two-thirty!" Juliet yelled after him. Then she groaned. "I don't think we'll ever get him raised! Well, why don't we see what we can find out about the mysterious artist? We can split up and cover different parts of town. I'm really getting excited about this!"

Juliet gave the girls their assignments and then started off. She stationed herself down at the town square, where many of the statues had ugly things painted on them. She put on dark sunglasses and pulled out a *Kids Magazine* from the case on her bicycle. Sitting down by the fountain, she pretended to read.

She always enjoyed being in the town square. Today the sunshine filtered down through the leaves of the huge trees. The fountain contained big goldfish that shone like the gold they were named after. She had brought some bread for them. She tossed it into the pool and watched them gobble it up.

From time to time she took out her notebook and wrote in it when an idea struck her. She had a dozen notebooks like this at home already, going all the way back to when she could barely write. When Joe asked her about them, she'd said, "One day I may want to write the story of my life. Then I'll have all the information I need." Joe had teased her about her notebooks ever since.

Time passed slowly. The town square became crowded. Children dabbled in the fountain. Mothers with babies in carriages strolled by. Some little boys were playing a game with a tiny football. They fell over each other and screamed. The square was a nice place—a little noisy, but that was OK with Juliet.

Finally she got up and just began to follow people. For a time she trailed a woman who was carrying a small paper bag. She was wearing worn clothing. Juliet thought she looked suspicious.

Then the woman went into a door of a two-story apartment house, and Juliet looked for someone else to watch.

For a time she watched an elderly woman sitting on a bench. Two little boys sat on each side of her, and Juliet figured she was a grandmother. She was reading a book to the boys, and Juliet smiled. *I don't think that lady is the mysterious artist or that she's putting bad pictures on walls.* She moved along.

She watched two men sitting in front of the hardware store. They were playing checkers, using an old wooden barrel for a table. They were talking about when they were in some war. Both of them looked fairly safe.

Time passed, and Juliet was getting tired. She decided to start back. And as she did, she came to the junkyard.

Actually Juliet had always been a little afraid of the junkyard. It was on the edge of a rough part of town. All around it was an old wooden fence. Holes had been knocked into the fence, but they were patched over with old boards and pieces of plywood. Juliet looked over her shoulder nervously to see if anyone was watching her. She saw no one.

Then she heard some banging and clanging from behind the high fence. She thought, *What's that clanging noise in there?* She kept walking along, slowly, and still studying the fence. She knew there was a shack inside.

Juliet thought about the man who lived there in the old junkyard. Everyone called him Junkyard Jake. People said he was a hermit. She walked along even slower, thinking about the man. She wondered what kind of person would live in a junkyard. She noticed there was writing on his fence, and it was very ugly writing indeed.

And then she stopped. She found herself thinking, *Nobody knows much about Junkyard Jake. He could have painted this bad stuff on the fence himself.* The thought startled her, and then she began thinking really hard.

The clanging continued, and she murmured, "What's he *doing* inside there?" She had no answer. It sounded as if he was banging pieces of metal together. *What in the world can he be doing to make so much noise? Sounds like he's tearing the place down!*

She thought again about what people said. The man almost never came out except to make trips to the grocery store. He kept a dog that had long ears hanging almost to the ground. Juliet loved dogs, but people said that Junkyard Jake's dog was a mean one.

Juliet realized then that she would be late for meeting back with her deputy detectives. She quickened her steps, still thinking, *I never had to solve two mysteries at the same time before. This is really exciting!*

As she hurried along, she tried to put all the pieces of the mystery together in her mind. It was a little like working a crossword puzzle.

"There's got to be an answer to this," Too Smart Jones said aloud. "And I'm going to get to the bottom of it!"

5

The Clues

Juliet found most of her deputy detectives waiting for her in front of the ice cream shop. But she noticed at once that one was missing. "Where's Flash?" she asked.

"Not back yet," Joe said. He peered at Juliet, then said, "You've sure been gone a long time. What did *you* find?"

"Nothing much."

Right away he rocked his head back and forth. "Come on, now. I know that look."

"What look? I don't have any look."

Jenny said, "Yes, you do. You look like you're about ready to bust. Now, what did you find?"

"First, you tell what you found," Chili Williams said, "and then we'll tell you what we found."

"No, I'll be last." So Juliet listened to all

their reports and gathered up all the notes they had made. "I'll take these home with me. Then I'll collate them."

"What's 'collate'?" Chili puzzled.

"Oh, it means sort of put them in order."

"You're always using those big words. Don't they make your head hurt, Too Smart Jones?"

"Don't call me that!"

"Well, they always call me Too Good Looking Williams," Chili teased. "I don't mind that."

Everyone laughed, but then Joe said, "OK, we told you what we found. Now you tell us what *you* found."

"Well," Juliet said after some hesitation, "you know that old junkyard over on the other side of town?"

"Sure. We know it. What about it?" Chili said.

"Do you know who lives there?"

"Some strange guy called Junkyard Jake."

"That's right. Well, the junkyard fence is all covered with graffiti."

"Not a big surprise. That's close to the tough part of town," Sam Del Rio said. "We found a lot of painted stuff over that way when we did our cleanup."

"Well, today I heard something banging and going on in there."

"Probably Junkyard Jake beating up on that dog of his."

"No. It wasn't a dog howling. It was like . . . like metal being pounded."

"So what's funny about that? It's a junk-yard!"

They talked more about the junkyard while they waited for Flash. They talked about Juliet's suspicions. Then she said, "It's getting late—we've got to head for home. We'd better not wait any longer for Flash. He must have decided to just go on home."

"Probably." Then Joe said, "Well, here we are at the ice cream shop. So how about us getting some ice cream?"

"I'm still worried about Flash," Juliet said as they stored their bikes in the bike stand. "Did he just go on home by himself?"

"Oh, Flash is OK," Chili Williams said with confidence. "I know Flash. He can take care of himself."

They went into the ice cream shop, then discovered that they did not have enough money among them to get more than small dishes of ice cream.

Joe ate his, complaining, "Why, I *spill* more ice cream than this!"

"Here, you can have the rest of mine," Juliet said.

"You sure you don't want it?"

"Not much. Go ahead and eat it." Juliet's mind was on Flash.

After the ice cream was all gone, they got

on their bikes and pedaled off in different directions. Even Jenny, who lived close to Juliet, had an errand to do for her mother.

"I'll race you," Joe said.

"All right, but give me a head start."

"You can have half a block," he said, "and that's all."

That did not help Juliet a great deal. Joe was one of the fastest and best bicycle riders in Oakwood. He soon caught up with her and pulled her hair, yelling, "Hurry up, slowpoke!"

Juliet gritted her teeth. She hated it when he pulled her hair!

Three blocks down the street, Joe unexpectedly turned off. It was not the way home, but Juliet turned, too, and followed him. "Where are you going?" she called.

"Just to take a quick look at that junkyard."

Juliet pedaled hard, but by the time she got to the junkyard, Joe had already parked his bicycle and was looking hard at the graffiti.

"This is pretty nasty stuff," he said as she wheeled up.

"Yes, it is."

"You suppose Junkyard Jake really decorated his own fence?"

"I don't know."

"He probably did. He's a rough looking guy."

"Oh, I don't think he really looks so bad. He just needs to get cleaned up and have some better clothes."

"You'd think Dracula looked good." Joe gave a laugh. "The gate's chained shut. Let's try to find a hole somewhere, so we can see through the fence."

They walked all along Junkyard Jake's fence, but any holes were well repaired.

Joe tried jumping up and catching hold of the top of the fence. Once he almost made it, but he was just a little too short.

"What are you trying to do?"

"If I could just get a hold," he told her, "I could probably get up and over."

"You don't want to get in there, Joe," Juliet said with alarm. "He's got a dog, and it's a mean one. You know what people say."

"I'm not afraid of any old dog." Joe continued leaping up and falling back. He always failed. "Let me stand on your back," he said at last. "Then I can grab it."

"No, I'm not going to do that."

"Then I'm going to get my bicycle. If I lean it against the fence, I can stand on it and take a look."

Juliet shook her head. "We don't need to be fooling around here any longer. It's too close to the bad part of town. Let's go home."

It took some convincing, but finally Joe gave in, saying, "If you were a brother instead of a sister, you'd give me some help."

"And then both of us would be in trouble!" Juliet snapped. "Come on. Let's go."

When they reached home, Juliet went at once to her room. She spread out the notes the others had made and began to read each one. It was the kind of thing she enjoyed doing. She liked to organize things and put them in order. Joe, on the other hand, never organized anything.

As she worked, Juliet suddenly thought, *It's funny how a brother and a sister can be so different. Joe likes to invent things, and that part of my brain is just about dead. I can do math easy, and he has an awful time with it. I wonder why that is.*

When she had all the notes in order, Juliet began to talk aloud to herself. "Let's see. The worst graffiti is on the west side of town. I guess that makes sense. It's a bad part of town, and the most suspicious looking people live there, too."

She studied the notes closely and murmured, "I'll have to admit the boys did a good job, even if they did go looking on their own." She was surprised to find a rather long note from Samuel. Apparently he liked to write. He wrote all about one interesting thing that had happened. His note said,

> Before we split up, we saw a small bunch of boys. They were about fifteen years old. We followed them until they turned around and asked us what we wanted. They made

fun of Flash in his wheelchair, too. Joe almost got into a fight over that. But Chili said it wasn't worth it. These guys looked suspicious, and I thought there would be trouble, but then Flash said to leave them alone.

"Flash showed real good sense that time," Juliet said. She laid a sheet of paper flat on the desk. Carefully she drew a map of the areas they had staked out. She noted where bad writing or rude pictures were located and what kind they were.

Then she studied the notes to find any descriptions of people that they had seen. The girls had done a good job. She read Jenny's and Delores's notes over and over. But, surprisingly, the boys had, too.

After a while she said, "This is making my mind turn into a whirlwind." She glanced up at the clock and gasped. "Time sure does fly by." She got up, gathered up Boots, and walked over to her window.

She saw Joe busily working in the yard. He seemed to be putting something together. She could not see what it was. "He's probably making a machine to bore down through the center of the earth." She grinned. "One of these days some of his inventions are going to actually work."

"Mrow!"

Boots was pawing at her shirt and trying to get her attention.

"Oh, you want to play, do you? I guess you deserve to be played with. You've been a good kitty."

She played with the cat for a while and wondered if he would ever grow tired of chasing a string. He never seemed to.

Finally she gave up and put him on the floor. "You'll have to find your own entertainment now."

She went back to her notes. She studied them. She tried to find some kind of pattern. There didn't seem to be any.

Juliet decided she had done all she could with the notes. She began thinking about the beautiful painting they had seen in the alley. She was pleased that the story about it had been printed in the paper. Looking up at the little bulletin board on her wall, she read the story again. "It's the first time my name was ever in the paper," she said to herself.

She walked back to the window and was surprised to see Flash rolling up the sidewalk. Joe was nowhere in sight, so she went downstairs to greet him. Flash could do a lot of things in his wheelchair, but he couldn't climb stairs.

Juliet went out onto the porch. "Hi, Flash! Sorry we missed you. We ran out of time and had to get home."

"I know. That's OK. It took me a little longer than I thought. Here, I brought my notes over for you."

"You didn't have to do that."

"That's OK, too. I didn't have anything else to do."

"Did you notice anything special?"

Absently, Flash reached down and rubbed the tops of his legs. "Yeah, I did. I really did."

"What did you see?"

"Well, there was this kid. He was maybe thirteen or fourteen. He had a can of black spray paint, and I saw him head down an alley."

"What did you do?"

"I took off after him, and I said, 'Hey, there! What are you doing?'"

"Did he give you any trouble?"

"He just laughed at me and said, 'I'm leaving my mark.' Then he ran away. I could have caught him, too. But I still remember when those bicycle thieves captured me. I didn't want to have any more trouble like that. Besides, the police weren't waiting to rescue me like they were then. So I just let him go."

"Anything else happen?"

"No. I just made notes of all the stuff on the walls and anybody I saw that looked suspicious. You really think all this looking is going to do any good, Juliet?"

"I hope so. But you never know."

"It's a real long shot," Flash said thoughtfully. "The trouble is that you can't tell by just looking at somebody if they'd be likely to write bad things on a building."

"You're right. And I've thought of that," Juliet said. "Sometimes even criminals look very nice, and some of the nicest people can look pretty rough."

"Too bad people don't always look on the outside like what they are on the inside."

Juliet was still talking to Flash when a strange expression suddenly crossed his face.

"What's the matter?"

He was rubbing the tops of his legs again. "Oh, it's just that my legs have been feeling funny lately."

"Have you been to the doctor?"

"Oh, sure. Mom took me a couple of days ago."

"What did he say? Did he say anything about when you're going to walk?"

"He doesn't think I will," Flash said and frowned. "He told Mom so. He didn't think I was listening. But I don't care what he says. I will if God wants me to. And maybe He does."

"Well, even the doctors say they don't know everything. What do your legs feel like now? Do they hurt?"

"Not exactly. They've got kind of a warm feeling. Burning, sort of. They didn't used to do that."

"Maybe that's a good sign, not a bad one. I mean, maybe life's coming back into them."

"I hope so." Flash smiled. "Doctor said there wasn't much chance of that."

"We have prayer for you every night when our family prays together."

"Thanks, Juliet. You're a good friend. Well, I got to go now."

Juliet watched Flash wheel off. She decided to pray for him right then. It had occurred to her recently that she didn't have to wait until prayer time to pray. God was always ready to listen.

"Lord," she said, "I know You can do anything. You made the sun and the stars and everything on this earth. So making Flash able to walk is really nothing for You. The doctors say they can't do anything more to help him, but You can. And I know, Jesus, that You just touched sick people, and they were healed. You even raised up dead people. So I'm asking You to come down and touch Flash and let him walk again—if that's what You want for him."

Feeling better, Juliet turned and walked back into the house. *Maybe someday soon I'm going to see Flash running down that park basketball court,* she thought.

6

Surprise at the Museum

The first trip to the museum at Collinsville had been such a success that Mrs. Jones and Mrs. Tanner decided the homeschoolers should go again. Juliet, of course, was excited about another trip. Joe tried to persuade his mother to take them to a ball game instead. He had no success with that, and he was in a bad mood for a while.

On a Thursday morning, the youngsters met at the church parking lot, divided up with chaperones, and loaded into cars. Juliet wound up in the Tanners' van along with her deputy detectives.

While Mrs. Jones was busy talking with Mrs. Tanner in the front seat, the boys and girls carried on a low conversation about the mystery. Juliet told them what she had learned from all their notes. She told them what she thought they could do next.

She must have gotten louder than she thought, for suddenly her mother glanced back and said, "What in the world are all of you muttering about back there? It sounds very exciting."

"Oh, just stuff."

Mrs. Jones made a face at her. "'Just stuff.' I'd like to know what kind of stuff."

Mrs. Tanner was driving. She laughed and said, "Probably stuff about camp or playing basketball or going on hikes or something like that. We know you kids."

Juliet was glad that Mrs. Tanner had taken the attention away from her. She whispered to her friends, "I'll tell you all more about it later."

This time the guide at the museum was an older man. His name was Mr. Michaels, and he seemed to know everything in the world about paintings.

They would stop at a painting, and Mr. Michaels would discuss the texture, the colors, and the meaning of the painting. He seemed very excited about his work, for he waved his hands around as he talked. He knew all about the artists too, and all that made the tour even more interesting.

"Much better than reading a book about paintings," Joe said.

Flash, wheeling along in his chair, was especially interested in one picture that Mr. Michaels said was painted by a man named Simms. That artist had had an unhappy life, and he'd spent most of his later years in a mental hospital.

"I'll have to say he painted pretty good for a crazy man, though," Joe said.

Mr. Michaels agreed. "Yes, he did. Strangely, it seems that he couldn't paint well at all before he lost his mind. All of his great paintings were done after he had his mental breakdown. They're worth a lot of money now, but he got none of it while he lived."

At last they came to a room that had not been open the last time. "This area," Mr. Michaels said, "is just for paintings done by local artists—painters who live around here. There are no paintings by well-known people in this room."

The children trooped into the special room. Most of the artwork here was done by people who had never sold even one painting, he told them. "They just liked to paint. They were strictly amateurs for the most part."

Juliet started walking around the room. Suddenly she stopped and stood dead still.

Joe ran right into her. "Hey, don't stop like that without signaling!" he said.

"Joe, look at that," she whispered.

"Look at what?"

"That painting."

Joe looked up, and his jaw dropped. "Well, if that doesn't beat everything. It's the same picture we saw in the alley."

Juliet murmured, "I just can't believe it!"

"But it can't be," Joe said. "They couldn't have taken that picture off of those bricks and put it up here. There's no way."

"No, this one is painted on canvas—but it's the same scene. See? The seagulls are the same. The rocks are the same. It's the very same picture. But it's here. How can it be here?"

As they were talking, the chaperones came along. Mrs. Jones looked at the painting and exclaimed, "Why, just look at that!"

Mrs. Tanner stared at the picture, too. "It's the one that was in the newspaper. It *is* the same picture, isn't it?"

"It sure is," Juliet said. "Now we can find out who painted it and how it got here."

"Sometimes artists sign their work. See if you can find a name on the canvas somewhere," her mother said.

They all carefully searched every inch of the painting, but there was no name.

Juliet saw that Mr. Michaels was talking with another group of visitors down the way. She waited until he was finished, then went up to him. "Mr. Michaels?"

"Yes. What is it?"

"That painting over there. The one of the ocean. Can you tell me who painted that?"

Mr. Michaels walked up to the painting. "This painting just came to us. Somebody found it and thought it would be good to display it here. It was found in Oakwood, but actually we really don't know for sure that it was done by a local artist. It could have been done by somebody living in another place, and the canvas just came to Oakwood. So it's kind of a mystery painting. A lot of people have been asking about it."

Juliet caught her breath. "A *mystery* painting!"

"Since nobody knows who painted it, I guess that makes it sort of a mystery, doesn't it?"

"It sure does," she said.

Too Smart Jones's mind was working rapidly. She kept walking back and forth in front of the mystery painting, while everyone else except Flash moved on.

Then she heard Flash muttering something under his breath. She turned to him and saw that he had that strange look on his face again. He was rubbing the tops of his legs. "Are your legs hurting you?" she asked.

"No, they just feel funny."

"I guess you don't mean funny ha! ha! You mean funny peculiar."

"Funny peculiar."

Juliet patted his shoulder. "If they're hurting, maybe my mom has some aspirin in her purse."

"No, I don't need any aspirin," Flash said quickly. "They're not really hurting." He rolled his wheelchair down the hall, leaving Juliet to stare after him.

Juliet never remembered much else that she saw that day in the museum. They saw a great many paintings and works of sculpture, but her mind was stuck on that one painting by the mysterious artist. Mr. Michaels told them that it had been found in an old abandoned warehouse a few months ago. No one could find out who did such fine work, which was rather strange to say the least.

All the way home Juliet was quiet, even when everyone else was chatting away loudly. She was thinking.

Apparently Joe had found the museum more to his liking than the first time. He even said, "It's kind of fun looking at paintings, after all. That Mr. Michaels—he knows just about everything about paintings there is to know."

When Juliet did not answer, he leaned over and squinted into her eyes. "Are you awake?"

"What—oh, sure, I'm awake!"

"I bet I know what you're thinking."

"I'm not thinking about anything."

"Now, that's not so. You're thinking about

how you'd like to find out who did that painting. Is that right?"

Juliet's cheeks grew warm, but she said nothing. She turned her head and looked out the window.

Joe kept picking at her about the painting, though. He asked her if she had any new ideas and even if they could borrow the painting from the museum for a while. He had all sorts of silly suggestions.

Juliet finally said, "Oh, Joe, let's talk about something else."

By the time they had gotten home, however, she had a big idea. As she got out of the car, she was thinking, *What we've got to do is go down to that alley where the wall painting is and stake it out. Every day. The artist might come by to at least see if his painting is still there. We'll just check out everybody who looks at it.*

The idea pleased her, and Too Smart Jones went to bed that night to dream about paintings and museums.

7

The New Painting

At first, all of Juliet's deputy detectives were excited about her new idea. Everybody quickly agreed to take turns standing watch over the alley. Juliet even made out a schedule so that, whenever possible, the alley was kept under close watch by one of her team. Of course, there were times when watching was not possible. None of the parents would ever agree for them to stay out late. That would be too dangerous. But Juliet would at least be able to find out what was happening in that alley at other times.

After nearly a week, however, most of her friends began to tire of the stakeout. Several of them started complaining. Even Jenny said she was tired of it.

"It's real boring, Juliet," Jenny told her.

"All you do is stand there and watch people going by."

"I can't argue with that." Juliet sighed. She herself found the stakeout boring. She had once read a book by a policeman who had become a private detective. One sentence always stuck in her mind. He had said, "Most people think being a detective is exciting. For the most part it is one of the most boring jobs you could find. You spend hours in a car waiting for someone to appear at the scene of a crime, and most of the time they never do."

Jenny was the first, but others began to drop out, also. One at a time, Delores, Sam, Chili, and even Joe finally told Juliet that watching the alley was just too tiresome. So the day came when Juliet and Flash Gordon were the only ones left.

All of this left Juliet discouraged. She asked Flash, "Are you going to quit, too?"

"Me? No. I never quit on anything. My dad taught me to stick with what I start."

Juliet smiled. She liked Flash Gordon. She had never seen anyone with as much courage as this boy had. She thought most boys and girls would feel like quitting if they had to live in a wheelchair. But he never gave up. Usually he was the most cheerful one of the group, even though he had the most to be unhappy about.

"I think you're going to make the best detective of all, Flash," she told him.

It was midafternoon, and they were on their way to have a look at the alley. Juliet had some shopping to do, and she was going to take Flash's place at the alley after she did it.

The wheels of Flash's chair squeaked as he rolled it along. "I've got to oil this chair," he said. "It's getting noisy."

Juliet glanced down at him. Flash was wearing white cotton gloves to protect his hands. His arms had become very strong from propelling the wheelchair. She said, "You've been praying to get out of that chair for a long time."

"Ever since the day of the accident, when the doctor told me I probably would never walk again." Flash nodded.

"It's wonderful that you have parents who believe that God can do anything."

"You're right about that. My mom and dad have never doubted for a minute that the Lord can make me well if He wants to. They're pretty special folks."

On their way down the street they passed a gang of boys in their middle teens. They were a pretty tough looking lot, Juliet thought. "Any one of those guys—or all of them—could be the ones messing up our town with their graffiti."

Flash looked the boys over. They all had

long hair and baggy clothes and were very loud. "But maybe not," he said sensibly. "You can't always tell by the way people look. A lot of the time you can, but not always."

Juliet and Flash had talked about that before.

Soon after they passed the boys, they reached the alley. Flash said, "I'll watch from here on the sidewalk. I brought a book to read."

"What is it?" Juliet asked as he took it out of a pocket.

"It's called *In His Steps*. It's a grownup book that somebody took and wrote for kids."

"Oh, I've read that. It's wonderful," Juliet said.

"I'm about halfway through it," Flash said. "Pretty interesting. Don't tell me how it comes out, though. I hate people telling me how a movie ends before I see it. Or how a book ends, either."

"My mom says that book was written a long time ago," Juliet said. "It's really helped me a lot. When I have to decide if something is right to do, I try to ask myself, 'Now, in a place like this, what would Jesus do?' I don't always remember to do that, though."

Flash nodded his head. "That's what I've been trying to do myself. Say, I think I'll go to the other end of the alley. There's some bushes there. It's easy to put my chair behind them

64

and still get a good view of everybody that goes by."

"I'll cut through the alley with you."

Halfway down the alleyway, they came to the painting, and Juliet cried, "Oh, look, Flash!"

Right next to the painting of the ocean was another painting.

This painting was of a tropical rain forest. Colorful birds flew in a bright blue sky. Yellow snakes hung from tall green trees, and a sparkling blue river wound its way through the jungle. Exotic animals were drinking on its banks.

"It's got to have been done by the same artist," Flash said quietly. "So he's still around here someplace."

"It looks like he is," Juliet agreed. "Mr. Michaels said there are art experts who can tell, just by looking, who painted a picture. Well, I'm no art expert. And I don't know this artist's name. But I'll bet whoever painted this one painted the picture of the ocean too."

"They look a lot the same. Same colors, same kind of soft look. Bound to be the same guy."

"Let's look up and down the alley. Maybe he left behind something that belonged to him," Juliet suggested.

"That sounds good."

The whole alleyway was littered with boxes

and trash. Juliet and Flash began to look close-ly at it all. They did not skip anything. They even went through some of the trash bins.

Juliet had almost given up when Flash said, "Bingo! Look at this."

She ran back to where he was poking through a trash bin behind one of the stores. He held up a can and waved it. "There are three of these in here! Right on top."

Juliet's heart leaped. "Spray paint cans," she said. "Do you suppose that the artist used them?"

"I'd bet on it." He pressed the top of one, and it still had a little paint in it. "This paint is the same kind of blue as the blue in the picture."

"Do you know what people paint like this?" Juliet asked slowly.

"Not really."

"I've watched people paint on T-shirts, and they do it with spray cans. They paint your name on your shirt, and then they paint a pic-ture if you pay extra."

"Yes. I've seen that. So maybe that's what this artist does for a living."

"Now we're getting somewhere!" Juliet cried excitedly. "And now we know this painter must live here in Oakwood somewhere."

"So we'll keep our eyes open for him. You go do your shopping now, and I'll hold down the fort here."

Juliet was so excited that she had forgotten about her shopping. She had to do it. She had promised to bring her mom some things. She walked to the department store, bought what her mother wanted, and then went back to the stakeout. She found Flash watching from behind the bushes across from the alley.

"See anything?" she asked.

"Not a thing. Nobody went into the alley. They all just walked past."

Juliet was disappointed. "The artist may come here after dark and do his panting," she said.

"Well, maybe. He might not want anybody to see him. But I don't see how he could paint in the dark."

"Maybe he uses a flashlight. But that would be hard to do, too."

Flash said he would stay and watch with her for a while.

Time dragged by.

Finally Too Smart Jones said, "I think we might as well give it up for today. We found out a lot, though. Take those three paint cans with you."

"I will. We can go by some stores on the way and see who sells this kind of paint."

They went into several places that sold spray paint and asked. Juliet was disappointed to learn that almost all of them sold this brand.

"That's pretty discouraging," she said. "If it was some special kind of paint, it would be easy to trace."

"Well, we'll hang onto the cans, anyway," Flash said.

And then Juliet thought of something. She said, "Let's go home by way of the junkyard and see if anybody's put any more graffiti on that fence."

"Suits me."

But nothing seemed to be on the junkyard fence that they hadn't seen before. Somewhere inside, Junkyard Jake's dog was barking wildly.

"He must get a sore throat from all that barking," Flash said. "He's not a bad looking dog, though. He looks better than Junkyard Jake does. But people say he's so mean."

Juliet suddenly stopped walking. "What's that over there?" she asked.

"What's what?"

"There. Right by the fence." She went over and picked up an object. Then she stood and held out her hand.

Flash leaned close to see what she had. Then he took it from her. "It looks like the top of a can of spray paint."

Juliet started to get excited about that, but then something surprising happened.

Flash gave a tremendous jerk, as if someone had touched him with a hot poker. The little cap he was holding went flying through the air. He grabbed his legs and looked up at her with a peculiar expression on his face.

"What is it, Flash?" she cried.

"It's my legs. They're burning again. More than ever."

"We'd better get you to the doctor."

"But it's not a hurting kind of burning," Flash said. "I don't know what it is."

Juliet studied his face. "Do you suppose maybe God is starting to heal your legs? I always wanted Him to do it all of a sudden, but it might take a while."

"That would be all right with me," Flash said. "However He wants to do it. I've asked God to make my legs well again, and if He wants to do it in one second, that's fine. If He wants to take months or even years, that's fine too. I'm just going to keep on believing Him."

Juliet felt tears in her eyes. She squeezed his hand, then said, "We'll just keep on praying."

As they turned away from the junkyard and toward home, they talked about the new painting.

Flash said suddenly, "We've gotten so interested in this mysterious painter that we've sort of forgotten about the guys who painted the bad stuff on places."

"That's right. We've still got to find them somehow."

"You really think that spray can top means

anything special? A lot of people use spray paint."

"I don't know."

"Well, we do know it couldn't be Junkyard Jake doing those pictures."

"Why not?"

"You can just look at him and tell that he isn't any artist."

Too Smart Jones did not answer. She was thinking of something Flash had said earlier about people and the way they look.

Flash went on to his house, and Too Smart Jones went to hers. She went upstairs to her room at once and began writing furiously in her journal.

8

Back to
the Junkyard

Juliet had become so interested in art that, when she saw a story in the newspaper about art classes, she became very excited. She rushed to her mother, who was in the kitchen baking a cake, and cried, "Mom! See? They're offering free art classes down at the Civic Center!"

Mrs. Jones wiped her hands on a towel and took the paper. Her eyes scanned the story, and she said, "Sounds like a good thing."

"Mom, do you think I could go?"

"There may be age limits, Juliet. You may be too young."

"No, it says anybody can come. Right here."

Mrs. Jones read a line and then looked up. "Juliet, you're pretty busy, but I suppose we could make art class one of your school projects. You think Joe would want to go, too?"

"I don't suppose so. Maybe if they had a class in how to make atom bombs, he'd go."

Her mother laughed. "You're probably right about that. Well, it's all right with me, as long as it doesn't cut into your other studies."

"Thanks, Mom."

"And mind you, now—you've got to stick with it. No starting and then quitting."

"Don't worry. I'll stick."

That was the beginning. Juliet could not wait until the first class. Two days later she was at the Civic Center right on time.

The newspaper story said that students should bring their own materials—charcoal, paper, canvas, paints, depending on whatever kind of art they wanted to do. Juliet thought she was not ready for oil paints, so she brought her sketch pad and plenty of charcoal pencils. She liked drawing but knew she needed more training.

The Civic Center was a brand-new brick building. It had floors covered with shiny gray tile. Juliet made her way to the big room that had been set apart for the art school. She went inside.

She was surprised to see all different kinds of people there. Some were gray-haired, and some were young, though Juliet seemed to be the youngest. She saw some people that she knew came from the wealthier families in Oakwood. But there were ordinary people too.

Not knowing exactly what to do, Juliet stood by herself at the side of the room and waited. Soon a man wearing a gray turtleneck much smeared with paint stood up. He had a jolly air about him. "All right, you future Michelangelos and Rembrandts, my name is Dickerson. My wife and I are going to help you all we can. This is Mary, and I'm Tom."

Juliet liked the looks of the two art teachers and thought they would probably be very helpful.

"What I want you to do is to set up and begin work. Mary and I will just float around and try to give you whatever tips we can. Take a break anytime you want it. This course won't be very structured."

"Will there be a final test?" an older lady asked timidly.

Tom Dickerson chuckled. "No finals. No grades. We'll try to help you, but you don't have to worry about a report card."

Easels were available here and there to hold the canvases. Juliet put her sketch pad on one of them at once and got ready to go to work. She started to draw.

At first she did not pay much attention to those around her. But when she finished drawing, she looked up, hoping to see Mr. Dickerson or his wife. She wanted them to tell her how she did. They were both busy across the room, however. She turned to the artist standing next to her and was shocked at what she saw.

There, busily painting away, was Junkyard Jake!

Juliet had seen the man only at a distance before, but she knew him at once. He seemed to always wear the same clothes, ragged blue jeans cut off just below the knees and a pair of heavy work shoes with no socks. Today he wore a checkered shirt that was too big for him and hung out over his pants. On his head was a faded red baseball cap with an "R" on it. He kept pulling it down over his eyes.

Juliet was surprised to see that he was much younger than she had thought. She'd always thought he was a very old man indeed. Actually, she decided, he looked to be even younger than her dad.

Suddenly Junkyard Jake turned and saw that she was watching him. "H–hello," he said. He spoke with a slight stutter, and he seemed friendly enough—more so than Juliet had expected.

"Why—hello."

"C–come to learn a little bit about p–painting?" His smile was timid but friendly, and that surprised her. She had thought he would be rather sullen and not friendly at all.

"Y–yes." She stammered herself and could not think of another word to say.

There was no time for more talk, anyway.

Juliet saw that Mrs. Dickerson had stepped up onto a platform, ready to say something.

"Tom and I are going to look at all your work," she said, "but first I want to make a few preliminary remarks about what it means to be an artist."

Juliet took notes on what Mrs. Dickerson said, but at the same time she could not help being much aware of Junkyard Jake.

To think he's right here beside me, and I can't think of a thing to say to him!

After the speech on art, the Dickersons began going around to the different students.

Soon Mrs. Dickerson came around to Juliet. "You've done very well," she said when she saw Juliet's work. "What's your name?"

"Juliet Jones, Mrs. Dickerson."

"Well, let me suggest a few things about your drawing here."

Juliet listened carefully and said gratefully, "Thank you very much, Mrs. Dickerson. I'd really like to learn to do better." She glanced over toward Junkyard Jake then—but he was gone!

"He's not there!"

"Who's not there?" Mrs. Dickerson asked, puzzled.

"Junkyard Jake."

"Who's that you say? What an odd name."

"Well, it's probably not his real name. He lives in a junkyard, and everybody just calls him Junkyard Jake."

"Oh, I know who you mean. The gentleman who wears a red baseball cap."

"Yes. That's him."

"I noticed him, but I didn't have a chance to look at his painting. That's too bad. I wonder why he left before I could see it."

Juliet shook her head. "I don't know, Mrs. Dickerson. He's sort of a strange man."

After this, Juliet packed her sketch pad and pencils into the case she kept them in and started for home.

She kept thinking how odd it was that she would run into Junkyard Jake at an art instruction class. Then a thought occurred to her. *Maybe Jake is the one that painted those pictures in the alley.* But she rejected that idea at once. For one thing, in art class he had been painting with a brush and not with spray paint.

"Anyway," she said aloud, "he's just too rough a man to make beautiful pictures."

The homeschoolers in the Oakwood Support Group had a new project.

Mrs. Boyd began explaining it to them. "We're going to do a very special thing this time, boys and girls. All of you know about that nasty old junkyard." She noted their nods, then said, "Well, the fence around it is just covered with awful paintings and terrible words. Somebody has donated more paint, and we're going to cover it up today."

"Hey, maybe we'll get a look at old Junk-yard Jake," Joe whispered. "And that mean dog of his."

Juliet had not told Joe about her experience at the art instruction class. She did not know why, but she felt better not sharing this bit of information with him or with any of her friends. For now.

The homeschool boys and girls and their sponsors arrived at the junkyard, ready to go to work. By this time, Juliet thought, they had gotten very good at painting over graffiti. The paint and rollers were quickly passed out, and Juliet began painting.

Samuel Del Rio was working beside her this time. He started off complaining. "I don't see why we have to paint a fence around a junkyard! I'd rather be playing ball."

"You ought to do what Tom Sawyer did," Juliet told him.

"Who's that?"

"He's a boy in a book."

"So what did he do that I should do?"

"Well, his parents made him whitewash a fence. When some boys came by, they made fun of him because he couldn't go fishing with them. But he fooled them."

"What did he do?" Samuel asked with interest. He was actually very good with his roller and was applying paint rapidly as he listened, rolling it over the ugly words.

"He pretended painting the fence was fun. He pretended he wouldn't give it up for all the fishing in the world." Juliet laughed. "The next thing you know, some of the boys were asking to try it. He wouldn't let them, though. He said no, he was too particular and besides it was too much fun."

Juliet dipped her roller in the paint and covered an area expertly. "And you know what? Pretty soon he was charging them money for letting them paint."

"That Tom Sawyer was a pretty smart guy. I wonder where Tom Sawyer is now that we need him?"

As the group worked, more than once Juliet could hear Junkyard Jake's dog excitedly barking inside.

Jenny even backed away from the fence a little. "Dogs scare me," she said.

"I've decided I don't think he's a bad dog after all. He just likes to bark," Juliet said. She had seen Junkyard Jake and the dog walking in town a couple of times. The dog did not seem to be as mean as people said.

"Well, well, you're all doing a fine job."

Juliet looked up to see both Mr. and Mrs. Arthur Boyd. They were the parents of Helen and Ray, and they were beaming with pride at their twins.

"If you keep on this way," Mrs. Boyd said, "we'll have this town looking like a utopia."

"What a utopia?" Samuel Del Rio asked.

"A perfect place," Mrs. Boyd replied.

"I see everybody's about done here," Mr. Boyd said. "Let's get things loaded up."

Juliet put her paint and brushes in the van and turned around to find Joe. He was not in sight, so she walked along the fence until she came to the corner. There, about halfway down the fence, she saw him. Her brother was bending over with his nose close to the ground.

Running up to him, she said, "Joe, what are you doing? It's time to go."

"I'm trying to look under this fence. See if I can see Junkyard Jake."

"It's time to go, Joe. The van's loading. Besides, you look silly there."

"Woops!" Joe suddenly popped up. He was wiping his nose with the back of his hand.

"What is it?"

"I didn't see anything but a big spot of brown —and then it licked my nose. It was that dog."

Juliet laughed. "He likes you! I told you he probably wasn't mean."

Joe grinned. "Well, you know what they say."

"What do they say?" Juliet asked as they hurried back toward the van.

"They say you can always trust a man that dogs like."

9

Patience Pays Off

As usual, Joe seemed to be having trouble with his studies. Juliet knew her brother was bright enough to do anything in the way of school subjects. That was not the problem. He was just so interested in making things and in new inventions that he simply would not give the time to it.

"Hey, Juliet, help me write this paper, will you?"

Juliet looked up from her art book. She had become very interested in art. She had begun to wonder if maybe she might become an artist someday. She saw that Joe's desk was covered with parts from an airplane that he was putting together.

"Joe, you spent all morning working on that airplane. You know you should have written the paper. You could have been finished by now!"

"Aw, working on the airplane's more fun." He grinned at her. "Come on and give me some help."

"No, I won't. If you couldn't do it, it would be different. You've just got to learn how to manage your time better."

Juliet ignored Joe's protests, got up, and gathered her art materials together. "It's time for my art lesson anyway."

"What's more important—your brother or your art lessons?"

"You are," Juliet said. "But I wouldn't really be helping you if I wrote your paper for you."

"I'm not asking you to write it for me. Just give me a few ideas."

Juliet was exasperated. "Joe, you have more ideas than any human being I've ever known! Now all you have to do is learn how to concentrate on your work. Then you can play with your airplanes."

She left the house, telling her mother that she would be back right after the art lesson.

When she got to the art class, she went at once to her easel and then kept an eye out for Junkyard Jake. She'd noticed that he always came in late, so she did not really expect him yet. She had also noticed that the strange man didn't really need art instruction. He was by far the best student in the class. Mrs. Dickerson had once told Juliet, "He ought to be giving *us* lessons." She had smiled then. "He is really talented. Never mind what he may look like on the outside."

About twenty minutes after Juliet started work, she saw Junkyard Jake come in. His clothes were scruffy looking as usual, and the red baseball cap was pulled down over his eyes. Dark brown hair hung out from under it.

He needs a haircut, Juliet thought. *It's funny —he's always clean enough and shaved, but he never seems to cut his hair.*

"Hello," she said as the man went to the easel next to hers.

"Hello, there." Jake rarely said more than that.

"Did you bring your dog with you today?"

"Nope. They wouldn't let me bring him in here."

"I don't have a dog, but I've got a cat. His name is Boots."

"My dog's name is Rembrandt."

"I'll bet you named him after an artist."

Jake just nodded and then went to work.

He seems so shy, Juliet thought. She wished she knew more about his family and about where he came from.

She continued to work on her drawing. She decided that it was getting better all the time.

As the morning went on, Jake did not say another word to her. His canvas was by the window, and it was turned so that she could see only the back of it. *What is he painting now?* she wondered.

Finally, she put down her pencil, walked over to the window, and pretended to look out. When she turned around and saw his painting, she was amazed.

"Why, that's beautiful!" she cried without meaning to.

Jake looked around, and his face turned red. "It's OK, I guess."

The picture was an outdoor scene. A meadow was full of wildflowers, and Juliet knew enough about wildflowers to know that they truly looked like that.

"That's a black-eyed Susan," she said. "And that's a jack-in-the-pulpit."

"You know your flowers," Jake mumbled.

Juliet moved closer. "They look so real, you can almost smell them. I'd like to reach out and pick one, Jake."

Junkyard Jake seemed almost frightened by her attention. He clamped his lips together and continued painting and did not say another word. He left early, as usual, so Juliet did not have a chance to talk to him again.

As she finished her work for the day, Mr. Dickerson walked by. "Juliet, you're getting better all the time. I've got a couple of books that might help you. Just bring them back next time."

"Why, thank you, Mr. Dickerson. I appreciate that."

Juliet took the books, put them in her satchel with her art supplies, and started home. She was still thinking about Junkyard Jake and how strange it was that someone who looked so bad could paint so well.

But she had been reading a book about artists. One of the things she remembered was that great artists sometimes were very careless about other things, including what they wore and what they ate.

Juliet was thinking, *Jake is like that. If he had a haircut and clothes that weren't so sloppy, he'd probably look nice.*

Suddenly she heard a whirring behind her and looked back to see Flash coming full speed toward her in his wheelchair.

"Juliet, we've got to get down to the police station!"

"What is it, Flash?"

"There's a bunch of kids, and they're putting graffiti on that new building over on Pine Street. I want to tell Chief Bender."

"I'll go with you," Juliet said.

They raced away, fairly flying toward the police station, two blocks away.

"You go in and tell him," Flash said, stopping his wheelchair. "I'll wait here."

Juliet burst into the station and found Chief Bender at his desk. He looked up with a startled expression. "What's the matter with you?"

"Flash saw them! They're messing up the new building over on Pine Street."

"Who? The graffiti guys? I'll take care of that."

Chief Bender was a big man, but he moved fast when he wanted to. He called to his deputy, and the two of them ran to their squad car.

Juliet and Flash hurried down the sidewalk after them. They got to Pine Street just in time to see the chief and his deputy putting some teenage boys in the car.

The chief saw Juliet and Flash coming. He gave them a smile and said, "Congratulations, Flash. You did a good job. We need more alert citizens like you."

"You'll have to give the credit to Too Smart Jones, Chief," Flash said.

"How's that?" Chief Bender asked.

Flash told him that Juliet had organized watching the alley and looking for clues. "I wouldn't have been looking for the graffiti guys if it hadn't been for her."

"Well, now, that's interesting," a voice said.

They all turned to see that Ralph Maddox, the editor of the local newspaper, had been standing there listening. A camera hung from around his neck. He took out a pencil and notebook and said, "Miss Jones, I would very much like to interview you and your friend here."

"You're going to put this in the paper!" Juliet gasped.

"I certainly am. Maybe it will encourage other citizens to be more alert."

Juliet and Flash happily answered all of Mr. Maddox's questions. Then he snapped his notebook shut, shook hands with everybody, and said, "It will be in the paper tomorrow morning. Hot off the press."

"Wow, we'll be famous!" Flash whooped as the two of them started toward home.

"You really deserve all the credit, Flash. You're the one who caught them spray painting."

"But you started us watching. I guess it doesn't matter who gets the credit, though," Flash said. "Maybe this will be a lesson to some of the other guys who are doing stuff like this. The guys the chief arrested aren't the only ones, I'm pretty sure."

The next morning Juliet could hardly eat breakfast because she was so excited.

Finally her dad said, "What's the matter with you, Juliet? You act like a worm in hot ashes."

At that moment, Juliet heard the newspaper thump on the porch. "I'll get it," she cried and jumped up from the table.

"What's the matter with that girl?" Mr. Jones said.

"I have no idea," she heard her mom say. "Do you know anything, Joe?"

"Nope. She's just being crazy like always."

"Don't talk that way about your sister."

"Well, she's real strange sometimes. You have to admit that."

Then Juliet was back, staring at the newspaper as she came. "Look at this. Flash and I are on the front page!"

She spread the paper on the table, and her parents and Joe gathered around to stare down at it. The headline said, "Youthful Detectives Foil Graffiti Experts." And there was the picture of Juliet and Flash that Mr. Maddox had taken of them.

"Why, Juliet, you didn't say a thing about this last night," her dad said. He reached over and hugged her. "I'm mighty proud of my girl."

Joe started to read the story out loud. His eyes were big with excitement.

> Quick action and patience on the part of two of our younger citizens have paid off. Miss Juliet Jones and Mr. Melvin Gordon alerted the police to the activities of the gang that has been defacing public property . . .

When Joe finished the story, he just looked at Juliet. Then he said, "I guess I'll have to say I've got the smartest sister in the whole world."

Juliet flushed. "Really, it was Flash who did it."

"Flash is a fine boy," Mrs. Jones said. "It's just sad that he had that terrible accident. But he always has such a good attitude about everything."

Juliet was still looking at the picture of Flash and herself. She said, "Flash is real nice, all right. And he still keeps saying God's going to get him out of that wheelchair someday—if He wants to."

Mr. Jones said, "Why don't we pray for Flash right now and ask Jesus to do that quickly."

They all joined hands then, bowed their heads, and then took turns praying that the Lord would do what was the very best for Flash.

After breakfast, people began telephoning. Everybody wanted to congratulate Juliet on the story in the paper.

She called Flash when the telephone was free, and he had not even seen the paper. She had to read the story to him over the phone. When she finished, she laughed and said, "We may have to start a detective agency, Flash."

"That would be all right with me," he said. "I like being famous."

10

A Different Kind of Graffiti

Juliet, I've got to talk with you."

"Sure. What is it, Mom?" Juliet was helping her mother in the kitchen. She had just put biscuits in the oven. Now she turned around and wiped her hands on her apron.

"Here—let's you and I sit down and have a cup of tea while we're waiting," Mrs. Jones said.

Juliet and Joe's mother had lived in England for a while and had picked up the tea drinking habit there. The rest of the family had learned to like it, too. The two of them were soon sitting at the dinette table and sipping the hot tea cautiously.

"Is something wrong, Mom?" Juliet thought her mother looked a little worried.

"Not *wrong* exactly. It's just that I think you need to be very careful, Juliet."

That really troubled Juliet. She never liked to displease her parents. "What have I done, Mom?"

"Your father and I were very pleased that you were able to help do something about the graffiti in town. It was a wonderful thing, and we're all pleased with the results. You have talent for things like that."

"But that's not all you've got on your mind, is it, Mom?" Juliet asked shrewdly.

Mrs. Jones hesitated, then she said, "I'm just a little concerned about something."

"Just come out with it, Mom. I can take it."

"First, your father and I don't think it was wise of you to be spending so much time in that rough part of town, Juliet. We don't have quite the kind of bad neighborhoods in Oakwood that they do in the big cities, but that area isn't the best section in the world. We don't think you showed very good judgment by going there."

Juliet listened without saying anything as her mother explained some of the dangers of playing around in that part of town.

"I know you meant well, but I'm just asking you to be more cautious from now on. Use good sense."

"I'm sorry, Mom. I guess I wasn't thinking. It just never came into my mind."

"You've got a very good head on your shoulders, Juliet," her mother said. "Just use it. We've all got to be cautioned from time to time. I need reminding myself." She smiled then. "You remember how your father fussed so much at me for going out late one night to get money out of the bank ATM machine?"

Juliet giggled. "He sure did. I didn't know he could be so upset with you."

"Well, I needed that, and I learned from it. Now, that's all we need to say about this."

"I'll be more careful, Mom!"

"Fine! Now, how about more tea?"

After lunch, Juliet asked, "Is it all right if we go over and play at the Del Rios'?"

"Sure. You girls have a really good time up in that attic, don't you?"

"It's the neatest place. All those old dresses and hats and shoes! And jewelry too—all kinds! Did you play dress up when you were a girl?"

"Every chance I got," Mrs. Jones said. "I suppose all girls everywhere like to play dress up. What does Joe do while you and Delores are playing up in the attic?"

"Oh, he and Sam play Monopoly or go out and shoot BB guns or throw a ball around. Boy stuff. We asked them once to come up for a tea party, but they just laughed at us."

"It's nice that you have good friends. You and Joe run along. Just be back in plenty of time for supper."

Ten minutes later Juliet and her brother

were cruising along on their bicycles. Joe, as usual, was showing off. He knew how to pull up the front wheel of his bike and ride on the back wheel alone. He had even learned how to get the bike going fast, then turn around and ride it backward. He was really very good, Juliet had to admit.

"Look at me! I'm about ready to go to work at the circus," he yelled at her.

At that moment, though, his bike hit a pot-hole, and Joe lost control. He flew over the handlebars, turned a complete somersault, and landed on his back.

"Joe, are you all right?" Juliet came to a stop, dropped her bike, and ran to him.

Her brother sat up. He had a dazed look on his face.

"Are you all right, Joe?" she cried again. "Are you hurt?"

"Hurt?" He seemed to be trying to catch his breath. "Of course not. I did that on purpose."

"Joe Jones, you didn't, either!"

"Sure I did. I just wanted to show you how I could turn a backflip."

Juliet knew better. Actually, she saw that Joe was almost out of breath, and she was worried about him. "Are you sure you want to go on to the Del Rios'?"

"Nothing wrong with me. Let's go."

But she noticed that he rode very carefully the rest of the way.

When they got to the Del Rios' house, the first thing she said to Samuel and Delores was, "Joe has a new trick he wants to show you. He's decided he wants to be an acrobat with the circus."

"Is that right?" Sam raised his eyebrows. Both he and Delores had taken lessons and were very good acrobats and gymnasts themselves. "What's your trick, Joe? We'd like to see it."

"Oh, she's just talking," Joe muttered. "Don't pay any attention to her."

"No, I'm not, either. What he does is he rides his bicycle backwards, then he turns a backflip and lands flat on his back, and then the bicycle lands on him. He's very good at it," Juliet teased. "You should see him!"

"Sounds like a great trick!" Sam grinned at Juliet. "Let's see you do it, Joe."

"Aw, don't pay any attention to her," Joe muttered again. "She's just blowing off steam!"

Juliet patted him on the shoulder. "Maybe we should just leave the acrobatics to Samuel. Come on, Delores. Let's go up to the attic."

As always, she and Delores had a lot of fun up there. Grandfather Del Rio had fixed them up with a table and chairs and a full-length mirror. Now they could have tea parties and look at themselves in the mirror.

Today, Juliet first put on her favorite—a white satin dress with a long train. She found a pair of ruby red high-heeled shoes to wear. And there was a box full of old jewelry, so she draped strands of artificial pearls around her neck.

"These earrings are so funny," she said. They had screws on them that fastened to the earlobe. They also hurt if she screwed them too tight. "They're beautiful earrings, though," she said. These were made of pearls, too, and they dangled down almost to her shoulders.

"My, if you don't look beautiful! Let me get on my outfit," Delores said. She chose a spangled blue dress that sparkled in the light. She brought out a pair of matching dark blue shoes. Then she put on a hat with a wide brim and an ostrich feather in it. She also found an imitation ruby necklace.

The two girls walked back and forth, preening in front of the mirror. Then they sat down at the table and had tea. It was actually only Coca Cola, but they pretended it was tea.

"I don't see why the boys don't like doing this," Delores said. "It's so much fun!"

"Oh, I think they'd like it if we had some clothes up here like Star Wars or maybe cowboys." Juliet giggled. "They wouldn't look very good in these dresses."

When the girls went downstairs later, they found Joe and Samuel talking excitedly.

"What are you two so excited about?" Juliet asked.

"Chili Williams just came by. He's going to have his picture in the paper, too. He saw another kid spray painting the wall of some store, and he told Chief Bender about it."

"Did he really!" Juliet exclaimed. "Tell us what happened."

"Well, everybody's been watching for the people who do this bad graffiti. And Chili saw this kid spray painting with black paint on this brick wall. He just ran around and told Chief Bender, and the chief went and caught the boy. So now another of Too Smart Jones's deputy detectives will be in the newspaper."

Juliet was so excited about Chili that she didn't mind being called Too Smart Jones. She clapped her hands. "That will be wonderful!"

As usual Mrs. Del Rio had fixed goodies for them. Today she served tacos and sopaipillas. She was a fine cook, and the whole house always smelled like fresh bread.

"I'll spoil my supper," Juliet protested when Mrs. Del Rio tried to give her a second taco.

"It won't spoil mine. I'll eat another one," her brother said quickly.

Sam Del Rio howled at that. "I don't think eating an elephant would spoil your appetite, Joe."

When Juliet and Joe started home, Joe said, "Let's go back by way of the junkyard. Maybe we can see Rembrandt again. I sure would like to have a dog like that."

Juliet remembered the serious talk with her mother that morning. *But the junkyard isn't really all the way into the bad part of town,* she told herself. *Just being close should be OK.* So she didn't argue with him.

Then they came to the junkyard fence—the fence the homeschoolers had worked so hard to repaint.

"Oh no!" Juliet cried. "Look what's happened to the fence!"

They laid their bicycles on the sidewalk and raced to the fence.

"Look at all that," Joe said wonderingly. "What is it?"

"I don't know what it is," Juliet pondered out loud. "It's not graffiti exactly. I mean not *bad* graffiti."

The fence they had painted all white just a few days ago now had different-colored splotches of paint on it. Just colored spots that formed no real picture. They were red, blue, green, yellow, pink—all the colors imaginable—and they were just scattered all along the length of the white fence.

"It doesn't look so bad," Joe admitted. "It's just . . . strange. Why would anybody do that?"

Juliet was thinking hard. But she didn't tell Joe her thoughts.

When they got home and told their parents, Mr. Jones frowned. "Well, it's still spray painting somebody else's property, even if it's not using bad words. It's a shame that all your good work was wasted."

"So what do you think it is, Juliet?" their mother asked. "Do you have any ideas?"

"I have one idea, but I can't prove anything, so I'll just keep it to myself."

Her dad suddenly picked her up and swung her around. It was as if she were made of feathers. Then he set her down. "You are a very wise young lady, Miss Juliet Jones. And you are just as pretty as you are smart."

"Oh, Daddy, you always say that!"

Mr. Jones kissed her on the cheek. "I mean it, too." Then he turned his glance to Joe and said, "You think you're getting too big to toss, eh?" He grabbed Joe and tossed him up, then caught him.

"It's a good thing we've got a high ceiling in here," Joe said, "or you'd bash out what little brains I've got."

Their mother was watching all this with a smile. "I don't know what you'll do when Joe gets to weigh two hundred pounds."

"I'll have to hire a derrick, I guess," Mr. Jones said. "But it'll be worth it."

11

The Statue

Juliet was sitting at a table with Chili, Jenny, and Flash in the ice cream shop. She hadn't seen Flash for several days. She had been wondering at the expression on his face, but she didn't ask him about it. She just asked everybody, "Have you all heard what's going on in the town square today?"

"What?" Jenny asked. "I saw a crowd down there, that's all. What is it? Are they getting ready for some kind of concert?"

"No, not exactly. There's going to be an unveiling of a new statue."

"A statue of what?" Chili turned his head to one side and said, "They didn't ask me to pose for it. It can't be much."

Everyone groaned and laughed at Chili. He was being his very funny self.

"It's a secret," Juliet said. "Didn't you read the story about it in the paper?"

"I don't read the paper. What did it say?" Jenny asked.

"Well, the paper said an 'unknown benefactor'—"

"What's a *benefactor?*" Chili interrupted.

"It means somebody who gives something," Juliet said impatiently. "Now, be quiet and listen. Anyway, this man who wanted to give something to the city gave it a statue, but the mayor won't tell what it is. It's a surprise. No one even knows who made it, the paper said—except the mayor. He won't tell, but he's very proud of it."

"Probably a statue of a deer or a famous man or a building or something like that," Flash suggested.

"I don't know what it is. But why don't we go on down and see? They'll be unveiling it in a few minutes. It's almost ten o'clock now."

"Wait! Wait! Wait a minute! Let me finish this," Chili yelped. He put his straw into his mouth, and there was a loud slurp as he finished off his milkshake.

"It's impolite to make such rude noises," Jenny complained.

"No, it's not," Chili said. "It shows you really enjoy it. As a matter of fact, there's people in some countries I read about who burp just to show how much they enjoy their food."

"You'd fit right in with those people!" Juliet told him.

"Shows what good manners I got." He stood up. "Now let's go see that statue."

The town square was only two blocks away. Juliet was pushing Flash's wheelchair, something that he very rarely permitted. As the boys and girls made their way down the sidewalk, he reached up and touched her hand. "Got a surprise for you later, Juliet," he said softly.

"What is it?"

He looked back and grinned. "It wouldn't be a surprise if I told you. Now, let's go into warp drive."

Juliet began to push faster, they all walked faster, and soon they were joining the crowd that had gathered on the large green square in the center of downtown.

"Looks like His Honor the mayor is going to make a speech," Chili said. "I hope it's not a long one."

"That's the only kind of speeches mayors know how to make—long ones," Flash said.

Mr. Wiggins was the mayor. The town was not large enough to pay a full-time mayor, so he also ran a funeral home. He was always dressed in a black suit, no matter how hot it was. When Juliet and her friends had arrived at the square, he was already standing on a platform beside a very large object draped with a white sheet.

"Wow, that's a big statue under there," Juliet whispered to Flash. "I thought it would be smaller."

"Sure is a big one, all right. Must be good if it's that big. What do you suppose it is?"

"I don't have any idea. We'll just have to wait and see."

Actually, Mayor Wiggins made a rather short speech for him. In his talk he even mentioned Juliet and her work in helping to clean up the city.

"We are proud of our young people, especially boys and girls like Juliet Jones and her friends. We owe a debt to them. And let all of us be more conscious of our civic duties."

There was much more of this. The election was coming up soon, and the mayor spoke favorably about almost everybody.

Finally someone in the crowd called out, "Come on, mayor, let's see the statue!"

"Ah, yes, the statue. I must admit there's only one disappointing thing about this work of art. It was donated by an individual who insisted that his name be kept secret. I am the only one who knows it, and I cannot be forced to tell. Now, I'm no art expert, but I think what we have here is something that this town will be proud of for years to come. Especially those in our public school system."

An interested murmur went around the crowd.

Then the mayor said, "Now we shall have the unveiling of the beautiful sculpture donated by an unknown friend."

The mayor whisked away the sheet, and the crowd gasped.

"It's a lion," Juliet said aloud.

Indeed it was a lion. Now it happened that the lion was the mascot of Oakwood High School. This lion was made of shiny polished steel. It was an impressive piece of metalwork. The rays of the sun lit it up so that its mane seemed to move in the breeze. The lion had its mouth open, and Juliet could see its teeth gleaming. Even the tail seemed to switch back and forth.

The mayor said, "Now Oakwood High has a lion it can indeed be proud of. It's made of stainless steel, so it will be here for many years to come. Why don't we have a big hand for the mysterious artist who has done so much for our town?"

Everybody clapped and then crowded around the lion. Juliet and Flash and Chili and Jenny waited to get close. It took some time, and while they were waiting, Juliet glanced around the throng of people. She leaned over and said in Flash's ear, "There's Junkyard Jake."

Flash looked around quickly to see—just as Jake disappeared into the crowd.

And then she saw Flash rubbing his lower legs.

"Has that funny warm feeling gone farther down in your legs?"

"A little bit." Then he said, "You know what I thought, though? About Jake, I mean."

"What?"

"I was wondering if maybe somebody like Jake could have done the nice paintings and maybe even this statue." But then he shook his head and said, "Nah, that couldn't be. Somebody who lives in a junkyard couldn't make a beautiful thing like that lion."

Juliet went up to her room when she got home. She took out her journal and began writing. Boots rubbed against her legs, and absently she stroked his fur. Finally she put the journal away and went down to supper with the family.

Her father had not been at the unveiling, but he wanted to know all about it.

"It's a really neat statue, Dad. It's a life-size lion."

"Really? A big one? You know that a real lion can weigh up to six hundred pounds."

"Well, this one's big all right, and it's made out of stainless steel."

"I'll have to go down and see that," Mr. Jones said, stirring sugar into his coffee. "Was it up on a pedestal?"

"Not yet, but the mayor's having one made —out of stone. And he'll have the date put on it."

"But the artist is unknown?"

"That's right. He's 'the mysterious artist.' That's what the mayor called him," Juliet said.

"Well, you must have some idea who he is, Miss Too Smart Jones. A smart detective like you ought to be able to figure out a thing like that." Joe stuck out his tongue at her.

"Joe, I don't want to see you do a thing like that again!" His mother rebuked him sharply.

After supper the whole family played a game of Monopoly—which Joe managed to win. He was a terrible loser but a worse winner. When he lost he sulked, and when he won he hollered. So, "Yeah, I beat you all! I beat you all!" he yelled.

"You weren't yelling like that when *I* won," Juliet sniffed.

Joe yanked her ponytail. She jumped at him, and in seconds the two were rolling on the floor.

"You two stop that right now!" Mrs. Jones said.

"Let 'em fight," their father said. "They'll work off steam. It'll make them sleep better."

"Now, you know that's not right, Mark Jones."

"Why, you and I might even wrestle a little bit."

Joe and Juliet stopped fighting with each other. By now both were laughing. "Make her wrestle, Dad!" Joe said. "Show her who's boss!"

Mrs. Jones grabbed a handful of her husband's hair and said, "Now, that's just enough of this wrestling foolishness."

Juliet cried, "I'll help you, Mom!" and she jumped on her father's back.

Soon all four of them were rolling about the family room floor. It was such fun trying to hold her father down. Of course, he probably had more strength in one arm than the other three had in all of theirs. But he pretended to be subdued and finally called out, "I give up! You win!"

"Let that be a lesson to you, Dad," Joe said, holding his father in a headlock. "You'll have to behave better, or we'll do this to you again."

On the way up to bed, Joe said to Juliet, "It's nice to have a Mom and Dad who can still have fun."

"Sure is. Can you imagine Mr. and Mrs. Boyd rolling around on the floor playing with Helen and Ray?"

Both of them laughed at that thought, and Juliet said, "Nothing like a great family, is there?"

"You're right about that, sister. Nothing like a great family." For once Joe was serious.

12

The Announcement

Juliet was disappointed when Junkyard Jake did not come to her next art class. She had planned trying to talk to him and get to know him better. But he did not show up.

On her way home, she ran into Sam, Delores, and Chili. She walked along with them for a while, planning the weekend.

And then Joe came barreling toward them on his bicycle. His eyes were blazing with excitement. "Come on, you guys!" he shouted. "You've got to see this!"

"What is it, Joe?" Sam asked.

But Joe was already off. "Just come and see," he called over his shoulder. "This way."

Juliet and her friends ran as fast as they could.

"I think he's headed toward the junkyard," Delores panted.

"Maybe somebody's done more graffiti over there," Chili said.

When they arrived at the junkyard fence, Joe was standing in front of it. He waved his hand at the fence and said, "What in the world do you think of that?"

Juliet gasped. The old junkyard fence had been completely transformed!

"I never saw anything like this in my whole life," Delores said softly.

The junkyard fence had been turned into a meadow full of beautiful flowers and butterflies and birds. It looked like rolling land with everything in it full of color and beauty.

Juliet was very quiet. Then suddenly she said, "It can't be. But still . . ."

"What can't be?" Joe asked.

"We've got to get into the junkyard."

"Why?"

Juliet whirled and wheeled her bike around to the gate. She pushed against it and said with surprise, "It's not locked. The chain's gone."

"Hold on, Juliet. We'd better not go in there," Sam warned. "It might be dangerous. Remember that dog."

"Let's just take a quick look," Joe said. "I'll go with you, Juliet. Maybe Jake and the dog are both gone."

But at that very moment a large brown dog pushed his nose through the partly open gate. His tail was wagging.

"It's Rembrandt!" Juliet said. She leaned over and patted him, and the dog reared up, trying to lick her face. "Where's your master, Rembrandt? Is he here?" She stood up and called through the opening in the gate, "Jake, are you in here? Jake?"

There was no answer, so Juliet poked her head around the gate and looked into the junkyard. Once again she gasped. "Oh my! I've never seen anything like it—not ever!"

The others crowded behind her until they were all inside, gaping.

The entire inside of the junkyard fence had been painted in the same way the outside had been.

"Only here it's like you were standing in the middle of the ocean!" Juliet cried. "It's so beautiful!"

Indeed it was. There were brightly colored fish, water plants, and all other kinds of sea life everywhere they looked.

"And over there by the shed—look at the statue of the dolphins."

The sculpture of graceful dolphins stood next to an old building that was shaped a little like a barn. *That must be Jake's house,* Juliet thought. They trooped toward it.

"Well, we've all seen work like this at least once before," she said quietly as they gathered around the piece of art.

"We sure have," Joe said. "Right away it makes you think of the statue of the lion."

At that moment a figure came out of the shed, and Juliet said, "Hello, Jake."

Jake stood in front of them, his clothes smeared with paint, his red cap pulled down to his eyes. "H–hello," he said almost in a whisper. He seemed embarrassed.

"I'm sorry we came busting in, Jake," Juliet said. "But if you'll excuse us, I just have to tell you what a wonderful artist you are."

Jake pulled his hat down farther and mumbled something.

"What did you say, Jake?"

For a moment Juliet was afraid he might turn and leave them.

But he didn't. He pushed up the bill of his cap and said, "Thanks a lot."

Sam said, "We want to thank you for that statue of the lion, Jake."

Jake stared at him blankly. "Nobody's supposed to know who did that."

"I don't think anybody else does know," Juliet said quickly. She motioned to the statue of the dolphins. "But you know what the art teachers told us. You can always tell an artist by the kind of work he does."

She saw that Jake was having difficulty making conversation. But finally he did say, "I'm not much good at talking with people. About all I can do is paint and make statues."

Juliet said, "You don't have to talk much, Jake. Anybody that can paint like you do and make statues like this—that's a kind of talking."

"You really think so?"

"Sure," Delores put in. "You just don't know how much pleasure you give to people."

Jake hesitated. Then he said, "Would you like to come in and have a soda?"

"That would be very nice," Juliet said.

"Well, I never have any company. You'll have to excuse the looks of the place."

He led them into the shed, and actually it was not a bad looking home inside. It was one huge room, filled with all kinds of paintings and statues. Off to one side was a small kitchen with a table and chair.

Jake said, "All I've got is Cokes."

"That's fine," they all said quickly.

As he passed out cans of Coke, Juliet looked at the artwork in his house. "You do such beautiful work. Like that lion. Why don't you want anybody to know who did it?"

"Like I said," Jake said quietly, "I'm not very good with people. Always been that way."

"That's too bad," Juliet said. "People would really like to know you."

"I get along with kids pretty well, but I don't have much luck with grownups."

"You'd like *my* folks," Joe said.

"I bet I would—if they're like you."

Jake seemed to be warming up a little, and Juliet asked questions to keep him talking.

He said, "I do a lot of painting of murals in other towns. Don't like anybody around here to know where I live. I let folks know once, and people kept coming around so much I couldn't get any work done. So I just moved here and bought this junkyard to hide out in. I can do my sculpture work here and nobody pays any attention to the banging noise I make."

"I did," Juliet said, smiling. "I wondered what was going on in here. And now we know." She said warmly, "You're just a wonderful artist, Jake."

Jake lowered his head. "Well, thanks. I'm glad to hear you like what I do."

The boys and girls did not stay long, for Juliet could tell that Jake was really not comfortable having visitors. They left, promising to say nothing to anyone.

As they were on their way home, Juliet said, "Now, remember this is a secret. You mustn't tell *anyone.* Not your parents, your grandparents, no one. It's just between us. It's the kind of secret that is OK to keep from the grownups."

"*I* can keep a secret," Joe said. "It's girls who are always blabbing."

"Not true," Juliet said. "Anyway, we'll all keep quiet."

* * *

For the next two weeks the town of Oakwood was surprised every day. Beautiful paintings kept cropping up on old fences and empty buildings all over town. Everyone was asking who was doing the work, and no one seemed to know. Except Mr. Wiggins. He knew, but he wasn't telling.

The mystery ended one morning, though, when the daily newspaper came out. Juliet brought the paper into the kitchen. She didn't open it, however, but gave it to her father at the breakfast table.

Mr. Jones looked at the front page, and the first thing he said was, "Would you look at this! So now we know who's been painting the murals all over town."

"What!" Juliet exclaimed. She ran to look over his shoulder.

"Local Artist Reveals His Identity," the paper said. And there beneath it was a picture of Junkyard Jake, standing beside the sculpture of the lion and talking to the editor. She read more. Mr. Wiggins had given Jake permission to beautify the town by painting murals here and there. And Jake had finally agreed to the mayor and the editor telling the townspeople who he was.

"I guess he got over some of his shyness," Juliet said to Joe later.

He nodded. "I think we may have helped him a little with that. He's really a nice guy. It's too bad anybody has to be that shy."

The discovery of the mysterious artist, Junkyard Jake, was exciting, and everyone at the Support Group was talking about it at their next meeting three days later.

Juliet kept looking around for Flash, but he had not come in. "I wonder where Flash is," she said to Jenny. "The Gordon family is always here on time."

"I don't know," Jenny said, checking the door. "But you're right."

Ten minutes after the meeting started, Juliet looked up to see Flash and his parents come in. Flash had a big smile on his face, and Juliet smiled back at him. He waved at her but sat in his wheelchair beside his parents.

When the meeting was just about over, Mr. Tanner said, "Are there any announcements?"

At once Flash Gordon's father stood up. He was a thin man with blond hair and light blue eyes. He was smiling in a way that made Juliet wonder what he was about to say.

"*I* have an announcement. My family and I want to share some happy news with you." He walked to the front.

"What is it?" Mr. Tanner smiled, too. "Are you inviting us to take a field trip to your church?"

"That would be great with me," Mr. Gordon said, "but that's not what our announcement is about."

Juliet thought everybody looked puzzled. Mr. Gordon rarely said anything in the Support Group meeting.

Then he turned to Flash and said, "Melvin, would you come down here, please?"

Flash began wheeling his chair forward, and his mother got up and followed him. He turned his chair around to face the people.

And then Mr. Gordon said, "I want you all to know that God has been very good to my son and to us. Show them, Flash."

Every eye was on Flash. Juliet seemed to have stopped breathing. Flash was looking straight at her and smiling. And then he pulled himself up with his strong arms until he was in a standing position. People gasped as he stood unassisted. Then he took one step and then another. Exclamations went up all over the room.

Flash started tottering. His dad caught him, and he clung to him. "Well, I took two steps," Flash said, "and I'm going to take a lot more."

Juliet's eyes filled with tears, and she let them run down her cheeks.

"God has answered my prayers," Flash said in a strong voice. "I'm going to walk again— and I'm going to run again!"

Everyone gathered around the Gordon family then. Flash kept on standing, braced by his tall father on one side and his mother on the other.

"The doctors told us this sort of thing does happen once in a long while," Mr. Gordon said. "We believe Jesus did it in answer to prayer."

Juliet wiped the tears from her eyes. Then she exclaimed, "Oakwood, you'd better watch out! Flash Gordon is going to be himself again!"

"Glory be to God!" Mr. Gordon said in a big voice. "Now will you all join me in a prayer of thanks?"

And the whole Support Group did.

Afterward, while the rejoicing went on, Juliet went up to Joe and spoke in his ear. "You boys had better watch out. Flash Gordon is going to be on the loose again. He'll run faster than all of you."

Even Joe's eyes were a little misty. "That's all right with me," he said. "I wouldn't mind getting beat by a guy like Flash." Then he said, "I hope I'll always trust in the Lord the way he does!"

"Me too, Joe!" Too Smart Jones said. "Me too!"

Get swept away in the many Gilbert Morris Adventures available from Moody Press:

"Too Smart" Jones

4025-8 Pool Party Thief
4026-6 Buried Jewels
4027-4 Disappearing Dogs
4028-2 Dangerous Woman
4029-0 Stranger in the Cave
4030-4 Cat's Secret
4031-2 Stolen Bicycle
4032-0 Wilderness Mystery
4033-9 Spooky Mansion
4034-7 Mysterious Artist

Come along for the adventures and mysteries Juliet "Too Smart" Jones always manages to find. She and her other homeschool friends solve these great adventures and learn biblical truths along the way. Ages 9-14

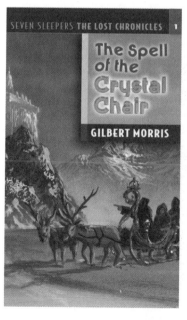

Seven Sleepers - The Lost Chronicles

3667-6 The Spell of the Crystal Chair
3668-4 The Savage Game of Lord Zarak
3669-2 The Strange Creatures of Dr. Korbo
3670-6 City of the Cyborgs
3671-4 The Temptations of Pleasure Island
3672-2 Victims of Nimbo
3673-0 The Terrible Beast of Zor

More exciting adventures from the Seven Sleepers. As these exciting young people attempt to faithfully follow Goél, they learn important moral and spiritual lessons. Come along with them as they encounter danger, intrigue, and mystery. Ages 10-14

Dixie Morris Animal Adventures

Follow the exciting adventures of this animal lover as she learns more of God and His character through her many adventures underneath the Big Top.
Ages 9-14

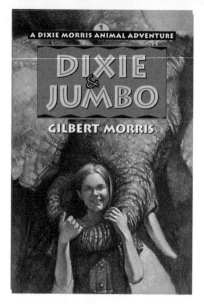

The Daystar Voyages

Join the crew of the Daystar as they traverse the wide expanse of space. Adventure and danger abound, but they learn time and again that God is truly the Master of the Universe.
Ages 10-14

Seven Sleepers Series

Go with Josh and his friends as they are sent by Goél, their spiritual leader, on dangerous and challenging voyages to conquer the forces of darkness in the new world. Ages 10-14

Bonnets and Bugles Series

Follow good friends Leah Carter and Jeff Majors as they experience danger, intrigue, compassion, and love in these civil war adventures. Ages 10-14

MOODY
The Name You Can Trust
1-800-678-8812 www.MoodyPress.org